Princess

Caitlin

Acknowledgements

This book is a gift of love to the world from a
deep spirit, Cathrin Ute Eisermann.

Friends forever, Donna J. Olson

Eric, Tonja, Evan & Erica Pohlman

Kathy McIntyre Blackburn

Klaus and Susan Wielitzka

www.mascotbooks.com

The Perfect People

For more information, please contact:
Mascot Books
560 Herndon Parkway #120
Herndon, VA 20170
info@mascotbooks.com

Library of Congress Control Number: 2016915851

CPSIA Code: PRT1016A
ISBN-13: 978-1-63177-748-6

Printed in the United States

The Perfect People

Written by
Cathi D'Avignon

Illustrated by
Chiara Civati

*I*t was just before bedtime when Caitlin's mother walked into her room. "Caitlin, it's time to get ready for bed," she said. "Let me help you with that turtleneck."

As her mother helped pull the neck of the shirt over Caitlin's head, she suddenly stopped and looked at her in awe. She bowed low and exclaimed, "Princess Caitlin of Hamilton! How wonderful it is to have you in our humble home!"

Caitlin giggled at her mother's silliness. Each time the neck of her shirt got stuck around her forehead over the years, her mother bowed and called her princess. And over time it hadn't gotten any less silly.

Once dressed in her cozy pajamas, her mother tucked her blankets gently around her and kissed her goodnight. "I'll see you in the morning, Princess Caitlin," she said and quietly stepped out of the room.

As Caitlin lay there trying to sleep, she began to think about how funny it was for her mother to have called her a princess. Or was it? She began to wonder what it would be like to be a real princess with a castle and a kingdom ruled by her parents, the king and queen. Before she knew it, she fell fast asleep and was dreaming of such a place.

*I*n a dimly lit library, surrounded by shelves and shelves, sat the King of Hamilton. He was leafing through a book, patiently awaiting Caitlin's arrival. He had summoned her regarding something very important. As she knocked at the door, he slowly put the book down and said, "Come in, my dear. I've been waiting for you."

As she entered the room, she said, "Yes, Father. I came right away. What is it you wish to speak with me about?"

The king replied, "Oh, my beautiful daughter, you have always been a loving and giving child. Now that you are older, it is my desire that you take a journey through the kingdom. The time has come for you to learn to know and respect your people, and allow them to come to know and respect you. For someday this kingdom will be yours."

"Oh, Father," said Princess Caitlin. "I shall leave at once."

"Wait," said the king. "There is another purpose to your journey. The castle is in need of some help. You must go out and seek the perfect people to do the following jobs." He handed her a list. "Assure them they will be paid high wages and enjoy the comforts of living here in the castle. Be sure to choose wisely, and offer these positions only to those who are right for each job."

"I will try," promised Princess Caitlin. She kissed her father's cheek and hurried out of the room.

*T*aking little time to pack, Princess Caitlin was soon riding in her splendid carriage down the long and winding road that led to many small towns that made up her father's kingdom. After what seemed like hours, the carriage arrived at a tiny cottage with the most magnificent garden blooming all around it. As the carriage came to a stop, an old man came out of the cottage to greet his visitor.

"Presenting Her Royal Highness: The Princess Caitlin of Hamilton!" proclaimed the coachman.

The old man bowed and said, "Welcome, Your Highness."

"Thank you, kind sir," said the princess. "I could not help but admire the beautiful garden surrounding your home. Is this the work of your hands?"

"No," replied the old man. "My son, Peter, cares for the garden. It is his passion."

"My father sent me in search of just such a gardener to tend the vast gardens of his castle. Please call your son so I may offer him this position," said Princess Caitlin.

"I cannot," sighed the old man.

"But why?" asked the princess.

"Peter is deaf. He would not hear me call. I am afraid he may not be worthy of working for the king," the old man said, turning his face away.

"Please, sir. The fact that your son cannot hear has no bearing on his worthiness as a gardener. I would like to offer him the job myself. Would you kindly lead me to him?"

It took little time for Princess Caitlin to communicate her offer to Peter. He graciously accepted the position of Royal Gardener. The agreement was sealed with a beautiful bouquet of freshly picked flowers, which Peter handed to the princess as she boarded her carriage.

Holding her flowers, Princess Caitlin sat back in her seat enjoying the comfortable ride through the countryside, stopping at each cottage and farm. Early in the afternoon, they entered a forest of tall trees. Just inside the forest sat a small house. The carriage came to a halt and from inside the house came a young man shouting, "Welcome, Your Highness! Welcome!"

The princess was amazed by the sight before her. The young man, who was obviously unable to walk, had built himself the most unique contraption. It could only be compared to a wheelbarrow. The contraption had a seat, and he was able to move by turning the wheels with his hands.

Realizing she had been staring, the embarrassed princess said, "Why, thank you for such a warm reception. What is your name?"

"I am called Ralf, Your Highness. I saw your carriage coming from miles away."

"But how?" asked the princess. "The forest is so dense. How could you see so far away?"

"My arms have grown so strong from turning the wheels on my cart that I am able to pull myself up to the top of the tallest tree and sit among the branches. I spend hours gazing into the distance, watching for visitors. When I saw the royal crest, I knew it was your carriage, Your Highness," answered Ralf. "May I offer you a cup of tea?"

"Thank you, yes. I have an offer to make to you as well." The princess explained to Ralf how her father sent her in search of a lookout and said, "I think you would be perfect for the job, Ralf."

"Please tell the king that it would be an honor to work for His Majesty."

"Oh, thank you. I will." The princess waved goodbye to Ralf as the carriage disappeared into the forest.

They rode on, and it grew dark. The coachman realized they would soon have to find a place to spend the night. There was a small town up ahead, and the princess arranged for a room at the inn. Hungry after her long journey, she went downstairs to the dining room. The room was abuzz with the whispers of the excited servants, all eager to serve the Princess of Hamilton herself. Before long, Princess Caitlin found before her a magnificent feast, truly fit for a princess, with enough food to feed the entire royal army. Making sure to be polite, the princess sampled a bit of food from each of the dishes. Feeling quite full, the princess turned to the attentive servants and said, "Thank you all. You have been very kind, and now before I retire, I would like to give my compliments to the cook."

Cautiously, the servants looked at the princess and then at each other. Finally, one of the servants spoke. "Your Highness…uh…Miss Winifred… well, she's somewhat of a grouch."

"Some say she's a witch!" said another.

"No one's ever heard her talk," said a third.

Undaunted by their comments, Princess Caitlin walked over to the kitchen door. She saw a woman hovering over several steaming pots on the stove.

"I am Princess Caitlin of Hamilton, Miss Winifred," said the princess. The woman looked at her sternly and nodded sharply her acknowledgment.

"The dinner you prepared for me was delicious. I have never tasted such wonderful food." Miss Winifred's face seemed to soften as she listened to the princess' kind words.

"Miss Winifred? Would you consider working at the castle as a cook for the royal family? I am prepared to offer you high wages and…"

Miss Winifred touched Princess Caitlin's hand to quiet her. Nodding her head sweetly, she accepted the position without speaking a word.

"Thank you, Miss Winifred," said the princess. "Now I must get some rest so I bid you goodnight."

The morning came quickly and with it came Miss Winifred's homemade hard rolls with fresh butter. Soon it was time for Princess Caitlin to continue her journey. For many miles the carriage traveled through the beautiful countryside.

Suddenly, one of the horses stepped into a hole and began to stagger. The princess could feel the carriage being tossed about the road. She held on tightly as they came to an abrupt stop.

"What happened?" shouted the princess to her coachman.

"I'm not sure, your highness…" he started. But he was interrupted by the galloping sound of two horses with riders heading toward them.

The two men bowed to the princess and immediately began to assess the situation. The taller man walked around the animals, while the shorter man gently stroked each horse's neck before looking further. Each man was, in his own way, trying to determine the extent of the problem. After some time, the tall man joined the princess and her coachman.

"My name is Michael, Your Highness. This is my brother, Ben. Our family owns the horse farm and stables up ahead."

"Thank you for coming to our aid, kind sirs," responded the princess. "What have you found?"

Michael spoke up, "One of the horses has gone lame. He'll have to be shot."

"No!" shouted Ben. "It could just be a sprain. We should try to help him first." Then he shyly looked at the ground.

"Your Highness, with all due respect, please ignore my brother," said Michael. "He is rather slow and does not understand the need Your Highness has for a strong and competent horse. This horse may never be useful again."

The princess thought for a moment and then spoke. "I appreciate your concern for our needs, but I would like to allow Ben some time to see how serious the injury to our horse is. We would like to stay at your farm until tomorrow, if you have a place for us."

"Yes, of course Your Highness, but…" Michael began, as the princess interrupted.

"After Ben has made his determination, we will make ours."

Michael stepped back and bowed as Ben began to wrap the horse's leg. Princess Caitlin turned and boarded her carriage, and they slowly made their way to the horse farm.

*S*pending the day watching the horses was pure pleasure for Princess Caitlin. As she stood at the fence enjoying their gracefulness, the lady of the house, Ms. Margaret, walked up.

"Your Highness," she said. "Would you like to join me for tea and cakes?"

"That would be lovely, but there is something I wish to ask you."

"Of course, Your Highness," Ms. Margaret answered.

"Your son, Michael, said that because Ben is slow, I should not listen to his opinion. However, I found Ben to be sweet and shy. He seems to care very much for the horses. Why would Michael say such things?"

Ms. Margaret considered her question. "Ben is a good boy. He never did very well at book learning and needs a bit more time to complete his tasks than his brothers, but he is truly wonderful with the horses. They seem to sense his compassion more than with other people."

"My father asked me to hire a new stable hand to work at the royal stables. I would very much like to offer the position to Ben," said the princess.

"You are wise beyond your years, Your Highness," said Ms. Margaret. "I will fetch Ben."

Upon hearing the princess' offer, Ben eagerly looked to his mother for support. She nodded to him confidently and Ben shyly answered, "Yes."

*A*s the day turned into night and the sun rose on a new day, Princess Caitlin anxiously walked to the stables to check on her injured horse. She looked in the stall where she had seen him the day before, but he was gone. As she turned, she caught a glimpse of a horse out in the paddock. As she drew closer, she saw Ben standing in the center with her horse trotting briskly around the ring.

"He's gonna be okay!" Ben yelled over to the princess with a big smile on his face.

It was at that moment Princess Caitlin knew in her heart she had made the right choice.

It was early in the afternoon when the horses were again hitched to the carriage and Princess Caitlin resumed her journey.

The road turned sharply to the left, and Princess Caitlin saw from her carriage window a crystal blue lake stretched out before her. They traveled along the road that wound along the shore throughout the afternoon. Finally they reached their destination: the largest town in the kingdom. The sun began to set as the carriage drew up to an inn. The princess entered the inn and gazed around admiringly.

"Aren't you the Princess Caitlin of Hamilton?" asked a voice.

Princess Caitlin turned and saw a sweet old man sitting behind a desk.

"Why, yes, I am," replied the princess. "I am in need of a night's lodging. Might you have a room available?"

"For you? Of course, Your Highness," declared the innkeeper. "Let me help you with your bags."

While leading the princess to her room, the innkeeper informed Princess Caitlin of a musical production to be performed at the town hall that very night.

"It sounds lovely," agreed Princess Caitlin. "I believe I will attend."

*A*t seven o'clock the curtain rose and the musical began. It was a quaint production, with the lead characters played by the town blacksmith and his wife. When the show was over, Princess Caitlin made her way backstage to meet the players. While she was complimenting the blacksmith's wife, she heard someone singing.

"Who is that?" asked Princess Caitlin.

"Oh, that's Daniella. Doesn't she have a lovely voice?" said the woman.

"Yes, she certainly does. Why wasn't she in the show?"

"She should have been. She came to every rehearsal and knows every part by heart."

"I don't understand," said Princess Caitlin.

"Well, it would be impossible. You see, she's blind," responded the blacksmith's wife.

Still amazed at the crystal clear tone and enchanted by the melody, Princess Caitlin made her way to the stage. She found a tiny slip of a girl and, next to her, an older woman. The woman whispered to the girl, and she stopped singing. They both bowed in Princess Caitlin's direction.

"Hello, Daniella. I am Princess Caitlin of Hamilton," said the princess.

"It is an honor to meet you, Your Highness," replied the girl.

"The honor is mine," said Princess Caitlin. "I heard you singing. You have a voice like an angel."

"Thank you," said Daniella. "I would have given anything to have been in the production but..." She stopped.

"Each year our family hosts a special spring concert and festival on the castle grounds. Artists come from all over to perform. Would you consider singing in the concert this year, Daniella? You could be my special guest. Please say yes."

"Oh, yes, yes!" replied Daniella. "It would be like a dream come true. Thank you, Your Highness."

After a comfortable night's sleep, Princess Caitlin awoke to a gloomy, rainy day. But not even the weather could dampen her enthusiasm. Today she would finally return home to the castle. After three days of traveling, she was beginning to miss her parents and home and was longing to see them both again.

The sloshing sound of the hoof steps combined with the tapping of the rain on the carriage roof made the last part of the journey calm and subdued. In fact, Princess Caitlin found herself nearly asleep as the carriage came to a stop at the castle gates. The coachman soon opened the carriage door and Princess Caitlin stepped down and entered the castle.

She was greeted by one of the servants who said, "Welcome home, Princess Caitlin. Your parents are waiting for you in the dining room."

Stopping to compose herself, Princess Caitlin opened the door and walked in to find her parents sitting at the enormous dining table. Going first to her mother, then her father, they shared embraces and sat down to their meal.

"Why Caitlin, you haven't eaten a thing," said the queen. But the princess couldn't think about eating. She was too busy sharing aloud the memories of her journey.

When she finally stopped to take a bite, the king said, "My daughter, you have made us very proud. You have grown in these few days and made wise and compassionate decisions. To celebrate your return, there will be a ball tomorrow evening in your honor."

"Oh, thank you Father. It is wonderful to be home," said the princess.

*A*ll during the following day, the servants busily prepared for the evening festivities. Soon the ballroom was filled with adoring guests, anxiously awaiting Princess Caitlin's entrance. All eyes turned as the words rang out…"Presenting Her Royal Highness, The Princess Caitlin of…"

"Caitlin, Caitlin, it's time to wake up and get ready for school. Caitlin, did you hear me? It's seven o'clock. Time to get up." As Caitlin slowly opened her eyes, she saw her mother standing over her.

"Here sweetie, let me help you get dressed. Do you want to wear the blue sweater or the pink one?" asked her mother.

"Blue," replied Caitlin sleepily, trying hard to wake up and remember the dream that was now so very vague in her memory.

When breakfast was over, Caitlin helped her mother with the everyday lunch choices—pudding or a brownie, applesauce or a banana. Soon it was eight-thirty and time to put on her coat and wait for the school bus to arrive.

Minutes later, the familiar sound of a rumbling engine announced the arrival of the big yellow bus. Caitlin's mother said, "Let's go, kiddo. Your carriage awaits."

Suddenly Caitlin began to remember the details of last night's journey. As her mother wheeled her down the driveway to the waiting bus, Caitlin shouted, "Mom!"

"Yes, dear?" her mother replied, as she turned Caitlin's wheelchair around to position her on the lift that would raise her up to the bus.

"Oh, nothing," sighed Caitlin, deciding to keep her dream to herself. After all it was rather silly for her to ever think that she could be a princess. Or was it?

About the Author

Cathi D'Avignon made a point of never denying her daughter, Caitlin, an opportunity, despite Caitlin's cerebral palsy keeping her in a wheelchair. Determined to encourage other people not to limit themselves, Cathi wrote *The Perfect People* when her second daughter, Danielle, was still young. Failing to find a willing publisher, Cathi shared her children's story with family instead.

She passed away from cancer in 2012, but she was an inspiration to many and lived her life by a philosophy of always reaching out to others. She touched so many lives with her kindness that friends and family alike gave *The Perfect People* a successful Kickstarter campaign in order to get it published.

She is survived by her two daughters, who are now adults, and her husband, all of whom are ready for the world to hear Cathi's story and message.